Sam.

4

I am Sam.

Am I Sam?

8

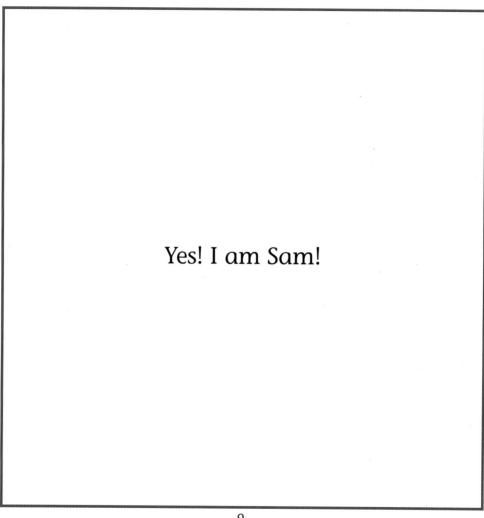

Yes! I am Sam!

10

Am I Sam?

Sam I am.

I am Sam.

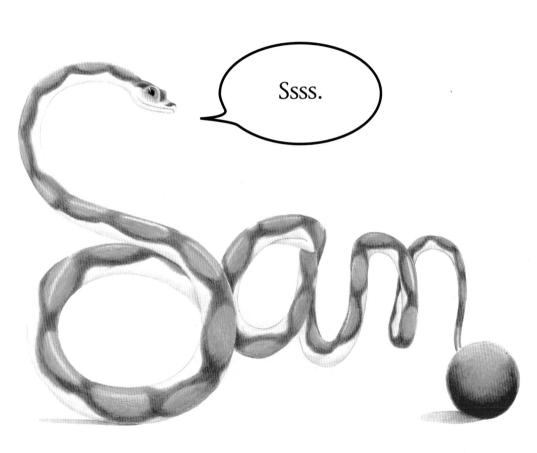

Target Letter-Sound Correspondences

Consonant /s/ sound spelled *s, ss*
Consonant /m/ sound spelled *m*
Short /a/ sound spelled *a*

High-Frequency Puzzle Words

I

yes

Decodable Words

am

Sam

Ssss